Tiny and his BIG ADVENTURES

A heart-warming story, with a "Tiny" bit of learning tucked inside!

Story By
Fawn Frazer

Illustrated By
Nate Voss

One spring day in Minnesota, three Chihuahua puppies came into the world. The puppies were white, with small tan spots, and each had a little brown nose. One puppy was much smaller than the other two pups, and the people called him the "runt" of the litter. This smallest puppy, in this litter of the smallest dog breed in the world, was named "Tiny."

Being the runt wasn't very much fun for Tiny. The other puppies were bigger and stronger than Tiny and they always bullied him. He never got to play with the best toys, was the last puppy to eat, and always seemed to end up with the worst napping spots. Tiny was so small that he didn't even weigh a pound when he was born. That's less than a large bar of chocolate!

Chihuahuas are a very healthy strong breed! For their size, their brains are quite large!

One day, something very strange happened. Tiny and his siblings were placed in a plastic dog crate and taken from their home.

After a long drive, Tiny saw that they were at an airport. Tiny had no idea why he and his siblings were there or where they were going. Inside the airport, they waited with strange people and heard strange noises. Finally, their crate was loaded onto an airplane, and before long, Tiny could feel the plane lifting high into the air.

Flying made all three puppies feel scared and worried as their tummies tossed and turned. After a long flight, the plane finally landed at an airport on the east coast. Inside of this airport there were new strange people and more strange noises!

Once out of the airport, the crate carrying the puppies was loaded into a van. The drive from the airport seemed short because the sound of the van's engine lulled the puppies to sleep. When the van door opened, Tiny saw that they were being carried into a small pet store.

At the pet store, the Chihuahua puppies were kept in a back room for a few days to make sure they were healthy and felt better after their long flight. From the back room, Tiny could hear so many sounds that he'd never heard before. He later learned that the strange new noises were other pets, like parrots, parakeets, doves, guinea pigs, rats, mice, hamsters and kittens.

Finally, the day came when Tiny and his siblings were taken from the back room and brought out front. They were put in a small puppy pen right in the front window. This was a small glass room with a gate into the store so people could reach over and pat the puppies. Tiny was now with other breeds of puppies... they were all bigger than him so he was still the "runt," but now he didn't feel safe and secure, just scared and helpless.

On that same first day, a friendly lady noticed Tiny
and stopped to take a closer look at him. Even though
the lady had owned and worked with many dog breeds,
she decided she wanted a Chihuahua puppy to keep her
company. The lady stayed in the store for a long time.

Many visitors came and went during the day.
Young children, teenagers, parents, boys and girls all
passed through, but the lady stayed and held Tiny close.
She whispered in Tiny's ear and spoke so soft and
gently to the puppy. Tiny liked the lady very much.

After a while, the lady decided
Tiny would go home with her that very
day. Tiny had found a new home! The
lady bought a carry bag, crate, leash,
harness and toys just for Tiny.

Tiny was so small that the dog harnesses wouldn't fit him - even the ones made for the smallest of dogs! The lady had to fit Tiny with a harness made for a ferret! It seemed like the perfect ending to a perfect day, but that was only the beginning of the adventures for both of them.

Chihuahuas have such small necks that they should wear harnesses, not collars. Their necks are no bigger than the top of an ice cream cone!

The lady loaded Tiny in her car and headed for her house. When the car finally came to a stop, Tiny looked up and saw his lovely new home in the countryside. Tiny liked the way his new home looked and was eager to start exploring.

The lady carried Tiny inside the house where he met the rest of his new loving family. The lady set up the bathroom with all of Tiny's new things… the dog bed, blanket, crate, toys, food and water bowls.

Later on, the lady took Tiny outside and they walked around the yard. They walked on the grass, around the dirt driveway, over the deck and under all the patio furniture. Tiny kept his eyes on his lady because no matter what they came upon, she always had calming words to help him feel safe. Whenever he felt too small, she was always there to carefully pick him up and hold him close so he felt like a giant!

Chihuahuas like some vegetables, and they love carrots!

Later that first night, the lady made Tiny some dinner of puppy food and cottage cheese. She sat on the bathroom floor keeping him company while he ate. There were no other dogs that got to eat first, no other dogs that pushed him away, but when supper was over, there were no other dogs to nap with either. Tiny's lady scooped him up and let him cuddle with her while she watched TV until he was sound asleep having sweet dreams of his new home.

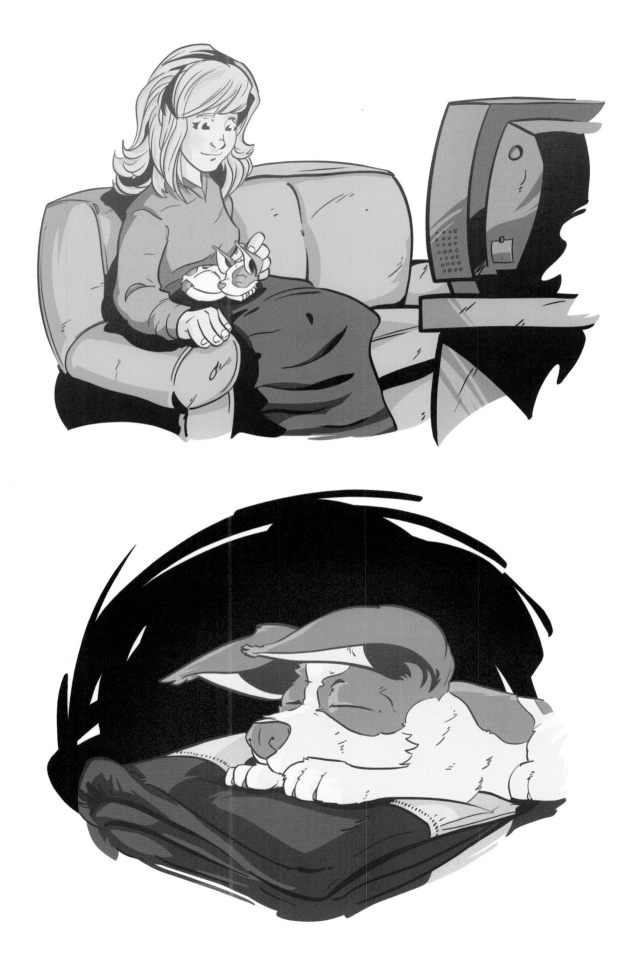

The next morning when Tiny woke up, he found himself all alone for the first time in his life. Being alone didn't feel good at all! His siblings were gone and the other puppies were back at the store. Where was his lady? She was gone, too! Tiny was feeling so sad that he started to cry.

Then the door opened and Tiny's lady was there to smile at him and scoop him up into her arms. She made soft "coo" noises and whispered that he was okay and safe, and Tiny believed it! He knew that he was home and she would be there for him every morning. Tiny would make sure to thank her with whines, skips and licks to show her how much he had missed her all night, and how glad he was to see her... and that's exactly what he did!

His lady's home was located in the woods,
but that didn't stop Tiny from finding the courage
to venture out into the yard with the lady. He
loved running in the tall grass and seeing so many
of his wild neighbors. Some were more noticeable
than others, like the turkey family — all twenty
one family members! Three mother hens and
eighteen baby poults.

The turkeys strolled through the yard three times every day and Tiny was very curious about them. Sometimes they would even walk up onto the deck and look into the windows. After their visits, Tiny would sometimes find a feather they had left behind and bring it to the lady.

Chihuahuas have no idea that they are small dogs! They will protect their person as if they were a huge dog. Because of that, their person must make sure they don't "bite off more than they can chew." When it comes to real big dogs, Chihuahuas will not back down!

One summer day, Tiny and his lady were outside enjoying the sunshine and the beautiful wildlife all around. She was watching over him from the shade because the day was very hot and humid. Tiny was right next to her most of the time, but occasionally he enjoyed venturing away from her in the warm sunshine. He could see all the interesting crawly things much better in the sunshine, but what Tiny didn't realize was that other animals could see him much better in the sunshine, too!

> Chihuahuas do need exercise, but because they are so small, playing fetch in the house with them is all they need.

Hawks' claws are known as talons.

Suddenly, his lady jumped out from the shade and stood right behind Tiny. She moved so quickly that Tiny got startled and turned to see what was happening. What Tiny saw next was so surprising he couldn't believe his eyes... it looked like his lady had grown her own set of huge wings! She stood perfectly still, between Tiny and the wings, and in the blink of an eye the wings went straight above her. That's when Tiny could see who the wings really belonged to... it was a huge Red-Tailed Hawk that had his talons out, ready to grab Tiny!

Tiny's lady stepped between the hawk and its prey and held her breath, expecting to be too late and to be struck by the hawk's talons! But in spite of knowing how much danger she had put herself in, she held her ground! The lady knew the worst place to put yourself is between a hawk and what it's hunting. But on this day, she had no choice, because what the hawk was hunting was Tiny! When the wind gusted upward, and she hadn't been struck, she scooped Tiny up into her arms and they went inside together, safely.

While driving to work one morning, the lady heard the radio announcer mention a photo contest for pets, with the winner getting a "walk on" roll for a play in the big city! The lady submitted a picture of Tiny, and with a phone call, the lady learned Tiny had won the contest!

The days passed quickly for Tiny and soon there was a big car waiting outside of his lady's company. It seemed to Tiny to be the time to be going home, but instead, Tiny and his lady, along with all of Tiny's things, were driven into the big city. Tiny slept so the drive didn't seem that long, and soon the car stopped and they all got out onto the sidewalk of the big city! The buildings were as tall as the sky and there were people and cars everywhere. Tiny stayed inside his lady's jacket and cuddled up close to her while she took care of everything.

At the back of the theatre was the actors' entrance.
There, people were in their costumes and rushing back and
forth. It was all so strange, but the little girl that would
be taking Tiny on stage came and patted him, which
made Tiny feel much better. Then, while the music was
loud and the lights were bright, the little girl put Tiny on

Chihuahuas are very good with children if they learn about kids slowly. Kids should learn about Chihuahuas, too. Tiny's lady had a granddaughter and Tiny knew the little girl was very fragile, so he made sure to be very careful with her. This made his lady very proud of him.

the floor and walked toward the open stage. Tiny was very nervous and didn't want to go out into the brightly lit area, but even though he stopped walking, the little girl skipped onto the stage, pulling Tiny across the stage as if he were a statue. As Tiny was sliding across the stage, he heard the audience say, "Awww!" because he looked so sweet and cute.

As time went on, Tiny and his lady had many more fun times together. His lady loved buying Tiny outfits to keep him warm when it got chilly or for the holidays. Some outfits were just to bring a smile to people's faces! Tiny had many outfits and although he didn't really have a favorite one, his lady seemed to like them all, and that was good enough for him.

Tiny was so grateful to have his lady! He knew the two of them would be together forever, and that their adventures with each other had just begun.

About the author

Fawn Frazer grew up on a farm in Temple, New Hampshire. She raised two children in Marlborough, Massachusetts then moved the family to Winchendon, Massachusetts. She's always seemed to find herself surrounded by wildlife. This is her first book and she hopes to share many more adventures with everyone.

About Tiny

Tiny is a real, live Chihuahua! Tiny's lady wrote this book based on all of the adventures they have had together — which are all true! She translated Tiny's feelings to share with everyone.

Interested in a Chihuahua? ADOPT FIRST!
www.yankeechihuarescue.org

About the illustrator

Born and raised in Lincoln, Nebraska, Nathan Voss has been drawing all of his life. His love of books started early as his parents would take him to the library every week to find new stories (early Garfield comics were a particular favorite). Over time, he stuck with drawing and illustration, eventually earning a degree in visual communication and design from the University of Nebraska, Kearney. He has been a professional designer and illustrator since 2001, working in Omaha, Nebraska. *Tiny and His Big Adventures* is Nathan's second children's book.